Acknowledgments

We all should be so grateful to what we are given and be thankful for what we have got.

As a ten-year-old I have been inspired by loads of authors that just make me want to read more. I always get my nose stuck inside a book, I just had a desire to

really write a book
and that's what
most authors do
too.

We all should take
every day as a gift,

every second is a Christmas.

As a ten-year-old I was inspired by hundreds of writers that just made me want to read. My top three were Adam

Dowsett, Jaqueline

Wilson and David

Walliams! Adam

Dowsett because his

book told me all

about the body and

made actually

understand myself

and he's my uncle.

Jaqueline Wilson

because she has

descriptive

adjectives in her

stories which are

just amazing! David

Walliams because
he's really funny and
I always try and add
that into my books.

Thank you to my
family – Anna, Adam
and Finn.
My auntie Sarsar
and my Cuncle have
really helped me to
make my books.
Thank you everyone.

I loved making these series and hope you enjoy reading them.

The Beautiful Escape Part One –
By Melissa Lillywhite

In an orphanage in London lived a poor girl named Tia. Her parents left her when she was two

months old. The

poor, poor girl

wondered the

corridors in dirty, old

rags.

The girl was only

nine, but her biggest

ambition was to

beautifully escape!

You couldn't blame

the girl really; they

were tormented by

the staff of the

orphanage. If they

would take two

showers in a day the Head Mrs Allie would give her one carrot for dinner! How mean!

Tia's room was shared with eight other people it was

crowded and well..··· grim. There were no maids to help clean and they didn't like it! One night, Tia looked out to the London skyline. The iridescent lights

beamed at her like a

stage. Tia inside her

head was making

the most daring plan

how to escape!

"Why do I have to

live this way?" cried

Tia. "All I want is a home with a family that loves me!" "Tia … don't cry. We're going to be alright I know it!" smiled Jade.

Tia crawled into her bed with dismay. She Squeezed her teddy tight, and she drifted off to sleep. In Tia's dreams she would sometimes dream about being the richest person alive. Or in her bad dreams losing Jade or Amy another one of her friends. But normally she would barley ever get to sleep, maybe it was because of the

screeching floor

boards or just the

beam of lights from

the stream of lights

in London.

DING DING DING!!

The wretched bell

like always woke the
girls up. Their yawns
were endless. The
bell meant that
breakfast was in an
hour. Basically, if
you didn't wake
up··· you would get

a smacked bum!
Now that was the
one thing she
hated!! She thought
if she had children
when she was older,
she would never
ever smack! So, the

girls got into their summer dresses as it was summertime. Then, they brushed their teeth. The girls would always help each other to do the traditional hairstyle

French plaits. Then, they would head to breakfast.

Tia knew tonight at around 6pm she would escape hopefully with Jade and Amy. They all went into the dining room in a line. "I have made a plan" smiled Tia. "For what?" asked Amy taking a handful of her wavy, short red hair out of her face.

"Escaping!!" chatted Tia. "Oh my word!!" says Jade. "Let's do it, who's in?" shouted Amy. "Shhh!" laughed Jade. "We're all in!!" said the girls. "Okay

meet me at are
dorms at 6pm , then
we can all agree on
a plan!"
The girls nodded.
Then they all went
up to the dinner
ladies and got their

porridge! Amy
looked with disgust
at the bowl. After
the breakfast it was
their learning time
until three o'clock.
So, their first lesson
was the boring,

useless assembly. It was pathetic all you do is listen to a person at the front. Today's assembly was speeches.

"Great!" said Tia as the thought of

speech's and
listening to Hermia's
voice always
bragging about
herself.
The girls all walked
into the ancient,
stone building that

was built thousands of years back. Mrs Allie stood grumpily at the front of the building. Mrs Allie was very pretty··· beautiful in fact. Her eyes were the

greenest. Her lips
were heart shaped.
But inside she
wasn't that
beautiful, she was in
fact ugly! She was
super mean!!

"Okay students! Time to begin!" Mrs Allie said while eye bawling everyone except from her favourite student Hermia Ellies.

"The first speech –
Hermia Ellies"
smiled Mrs Allie
happy to see her
favourite student.
Tia rolled her eyes at
the thought of
Hermia. She was so

mean but also so awkward, you're about to see so in this speech···

"Okay Hermia tell us about your speech!" smiled Mrs Allie.

"Hello, my names Hermia. So last year was amazing except for Tia Solee. She always came into my dorm and stole my clothes! That's why I came to breakfast once naked" said

Hermia. The whole

school burst into

chuckles of laughter.

Tia, Amy and Jade

looked at each other

and giggled. "Maybe

Tia needs to go to

my office? Tia do your speech and you may change my decision." Mrs Allie said in a stern voice. "Yes Mrs Allie!" Said Tia in a very nervous voice. "Okay Tia over to you" Mrs

Allie showed a weak

smile.

"Hi, my name is Tia!

Please don't send

me to detention! I

did not steal her

clothes because

everyone would agree that she is so much shorter than me! Also, why couldn't she come in her night gown? I also wouldn't do it because I have been here long enough to know detentions are horrible!" Tia groaned as she knew that she was going to get detention. But she wasn't even going to be here tonight,

so it didn't matter.

"Ok, the results will

come tomorrow

morning. I will

decide!" barked Mrs

Allie.

So, the day went on very slowly like a slug going up a mountain. Their lessons were art, PE, baking, music and dancing and so on. When the bell

went that meant that
lessons had
finished, the girls
were exhilarated!
The girls went up
the crowded
corridors with all
sorts of people in it

and found their

dorm door.

"Are we really going

to do this?"

questioned Amy.

"Yes! Just pack your

stuff before the

others come in to do

their homework

because they could

tell on us! And this

would never happen,

and we would be

devastated!!"

strained Tia. "But

what if your parents

don't want us? What if they hurt us! What if they.." Jade didn't have the time to finish her sentence before Tia butted in.

"Jade! Of course not, don't be silly!

Now pack your stuff and maybe if Amy could sneak into the kitchen and get us a few snacks from the leftovers of lunch?! stammered Tia. "Yes sure!" smiled Amy.

Amy walked slowly past Mrs Allies Office. Luckily, the kitchen was right next to their dorm. Amy went inside the kitchen and loads and loads and loads

of bottles of water
were everywhere.

"What's that about?
Anyway, let's get
three Mars Bars and
maybe water
because it's
everywhere?"

giggled Amy. Amy quickly got her food and then zoomed off back to the dorm. "Perfect timing! We have just got the rope tied and packed your stuff and everything is done!" smiled Tia. "So are we ready?" Jade said whilst looking out. "Yes. Three Two One!!" screamed Tia.

It took the girls about five minutes to get down the rope because the orphanage was one of the biggest and tallest in the world, it was named Betty!

"Okay guys! We're going to walk through London to Manif street where my real parents live!" smiled Tia.

"Ok!" giggled Amy.

"You sure?" Jade

asked slightly unsure. "Yes! Stop worrying and let's go!" Smiled Tia. They all went past the London Eye, Westminster Abbey and just opposite

the abbey was Manif
street!

"Yes! WE HAVE
MADE IT!" laughed
Tia. Tia went over to
a very luxurious and
rather fancy looking
house. "This is the

one!" Tia said while reading the address to see if it was the right one. Tia knocked nervously. "Yes?" smiled a lady who looked very nicely dressed.

"Hi I am Tia! Are you my long-lost parent? These are my friends Jade and Amy! I was wondering if you could maybe be my parent and also my friends' parent again? I know it's a big thing to ask but ..." Tia said while shaking.

Tia? Amy and Jade? You're all triplets, is that right? I put you

in the orphanage
called Betty just up
the road. You're all
sisters! I would love
to look after you
again so yes! I am
so sorry girls that I
put you in an

orphanage ⋯ I was way too young to look after you and I was actually coming to get you tonight. I have thought about you every day!" smiled their mother.

"So we can be a big happy family?" smiled Tia. "Yes!" smiled their mother.

The end of part one.

The Beautiful Escape Part Two –

By Melissa Lillywhite

Tia and her two friends (aka her sisters) had just settled into their new house. Their house was gigantic! There was a lot of spectacular stuff hidden inside this house. But let's get onto this story!

Tia had just gone to sleep in her new bedroom having just met her father. Tia, Amy and Jade would only see their father once a year. They would only see their

mother named Zen
only 4 days of the
week. When they
were alone, they
would be looked
after by loads of
nannies, maids and
guards. They had a

collection of staff –
cooks, drivers,
cleaners, maids,
guards, nannies,
tutors and even their
personal nurse and
doctor! But there
was one rude and

mean Nannie called
Eliza. The rudest
person of all time!
They always tell their
mother to fire her
but she wouldn't
listen.

DING, DING, DING, DING, DING!!!! Tia's horrible alarm clock went off. She needed to get up and she could smell the mouth-watering fry up cooking downstairs. She opened her door and Eliza's face beamed onto hers. "Brush your teeth you little twit" snarled Eliza. "No! You don't control me!" Tia growled.

"You will do what I

say you twit!"

shouted Eliza.

"You're being rude!

Go away I am going

to breakfast, and I

don't care if mother

and father aren't here! It doesn't mean you own me! My parents do!" cried Tia. Tia walked straight past Eliza and her red curly hair and snuck into

Jades room.

"Jade?" shouted

Tia, petrified. Then

she walked through

six corridors to get

to Amy's room!

"Amy?" shouted Tia.

They both weren't in

their rooms! Tia ran downstairs outside the front door and asked the chief guard to look for Amy and Jade! At lunch, the chief guard called Zej walked over to Tia.

"They are nowhere

to be seen!" cried

Zej. "What!? Jade

and Amy have

disappeared!"

screamed Tia.

"I didn't notice. Anyway, I couldn't care less, it's just as hard having you here, you can't stop being annoying, can you?" grinned Eliza. "We could look for them for a little

while— it's

something to do I

guess" Eliza said in

a very rude tone.

"Something to do!

Are you kidding me?

They are your

responsibility"
shouted Tia.

"Whatever! We can go on the train. Let me read out where they are on their tracker" growled Eliza.

"Really? Saint Paul's cathedral!" "Let's go!" said Tia getting her phone out. They both walked over the Millennium bridge, it was the most beautiful view she had ever seen! It had a sparkly and iridescent pop to the murky foggy water. Tia loved walking over the bridge.

"Now don't be an animal like you are

and stay quiet!"

shouted Eliza. "Well

you're not being

quiet" whispered

Tia. "Shut up!"

Barked Eliza.

They both walked

into the dark ancient

stone building, it was incredible. A big bolt of light from the sun loomed into the building.

"Where are these little things?" said Eliza. "Well, your

phone says they are at the London eye!" screamed Tia. "Are you kidding me! You are···. what the London eye! You ... fine let's go" Eliza screeched in anger.

They walked off the bridge and into a little neighbourhood and then⋯ "Look up" shouted Tia. "Wow that's magnificent!" cried Eliza. The circle was like a ring. The little capsules moved around like a sloth. "Look!" screamed Tia. "There!" "Ugh, ok let's wait⋯." yawed Eliza. After 30 minutes of horrible waiting the capsule that they were in came to a stop!

"Yes!!!" screamed Tia.

"Tia? Eliza? What are you doing

here?" asked Amy.

"No, what are you guys doing here?" cried Tia. "We're⋯ sorry" said Jade. "But what were you doing?" shouted Tia. "We were sleep walking" Amy said

uncomfortably as

she was lying.

"Well? Ok?" said

Tia. "No, No that's

not alright! You

twits! You both went

out! You little brats!"

shouted Eliza.

"We're sorry···"

sighed Jade.

Finally, they all went

back in peace. They

passed flying birds

and beautiful flowing

lakes. And then the

sun settled down
and it was time to
go to sleep.

The end of part two.

The Beautiful Escape Part 3 – By Melissa Lillywhite

Back home, Tia saw her dad packing his suitcase···she had an idea. Tia's father

had lots of bags to
pack. He noticed
that one bag was
heavier than it
should be. He was
running late so he
didn't take much
notice. He shouted

goodbye in a booming voice but didn't hear Tia's reply. "Where was she?" He thought. He rushed outside in scorching weather

and caught a taxi to
the port.

Meanwhile, Tia was
inside her father's
bag giggling to
herself. She was the
most mischievous of
the children. When

Tia's father named Jack set sail to Jamaica he looked on his phone and saw a picture of Tia. It really made him home sick, and he wondered why she didn't reply when he

said goodbye.

Suddenly, he heard

a little chuckle

coming from his

bag. Jack was

petrified at first, he

thought it was a rat

– his biggest fear.

Then he

remembered that

tone of voice when

he dropped the girls

of at the orphanage

9 years ago. He

suddenly ran as fast

as he could to get to

the bags. Unzipping

the heaviest one and

standing before his

eyes was TIA!

He felt shocked,

happiness and

puzzled as to why

she was on the ship,

knowing that no

family members are

allowed to step foot

on the boat as there

could be a war at

anytime. "Wh wh

what are you doing

Tia? H h how did you get into my bag Tia?" questioned Jack. "I snuck aboard to be with you dad!" smiled Tia. "Tia, I was missing you··· but ..

something could

happen. My captain

has his daughter

aboard so I could

ask him if you could

share a room with

his daughter?" said

Jack while looking at his captain.

"But father I want to help! This wrecked ship could use a little makeover." giggled Tia. "No!" shouted Jack. "Fine.

Ahhhhhh!"

screamed Tia

In the distance they

could see a gigantic

tsunami sprinting in

front of them!! The

tsunami was

growing and

growing like a child
to an elder but a
quicker version. The
blue, turquoise
water curled up
getting ready to hit
them. "FULL SAILS
MATIES FULL

SAILS!" Shouted a
Man in Blue with
weird golden tassels
on his suit. "I have
to go Tia, stay
safe!" cried Jack.
But Tia wasn't going
to let her father go

like that and she

quickly climbed onto

his legs. But if you

asked Tia she

probably wouldn't

remember because

the tsunami had

already fallen onto

the boat.

Underwater, Tia

looked for her father

petrified. Luckily, Tia

knew how to swim

but where was her

father? She

suddenly was running out of breath, so she went up to the water surface. But when she was up, they all had sailed away without her!

"Father?!" Shouted Tia catching her breath back. She saw a black figure underneath the water. For a few seconds it wiggled and wobbled until finally it came up

from the water.

"TIA YOUR'E OK!"

Cried Jack. "Do you

know how to swim

because you were

underwater for a

very long time!"

Shouted Tia as the waves were very loud echoing across the sky. "Yes, but I was caught up with some strange thing on my ankle!" Said Jack while clambering over another gigantic wave. "Well how are we going to get home?" Cried Tia. "We need to follow the ship, but it's gone so I guess we must go this way!

That's the only way

to shore. Luckily, I

have got my bag

with me so I can use

the money in my

bag to get a flight as

we are now in

Australia" sighed

Jack. "Ok? But I

guess we need find

a float because I am

not going to swim all

that way!" Smiled

Tia. "Yeah, I know.

So, you're going on

my back."

Stammered Jack.

For Jacks job you

had to be incredibly

fit so it wasn't going

to be hard for him.

The ride was fine

but occasionally

there was a tidal wave. Tia usually would get seasick but she got used to it after a while. For about 5 hours straight they were swimming in nothing, just water and the sky – that's it. So, the thing is that Tia was getting VERY VERY VERY bored! Like VERY! She found a game where you would

make your hands
into a triangle but
that's all she could
think of. Before Tia
was going to FREAK
out, she saw land it
was a very green
and luxurious

landscape that glistened in the sunset. Yes, it was getting to sunset! And bearing in mind they were on the ship at 6:15am!! It came closer and

closer beckoning
them to come and
enter the landscape.
Strangely it seemed
that they were in
South Africa. Tia's
father thought that

they would end up in

Australia!

"How strange⋯"

said her dad looking

puzzled. Jack knew

every single little

area in the role. How

could they end up in

South Africa? Tia was shocked and so was Jack, but they had to get onto a plane or at least get to the airport. Tia and her father didn't talk to each other until her father knew where they were.

"Finally, the airport!" Smiled Jack as he took Tia off his back.

"Well, I don't know where we are!"

Shouted Tia a bit
tired from her trip.
"Tia stop" said
Jack. "Sorry I just
need to get to the
airport" Howled Tia.
"It's fine ⋯ " replied
Jack. The airport

pillars loomed upwards and towered upon Tia and her father. "Wow! It's an amazing airport!! As I work in the army, I can get our flight for free!" Smiled Jack. "Right we better get home or mums going to be mad!" Laughed Jack while scanning his passport. Tia and

Jack when into the amazing luxurious plane that was full of people. And luckily from where they were, it was only two hours away from home! Tia was overjoyed when she

came off the plane

to see her two

sisters and mother

waiting. "Oh my

goodness me! I was

so worried! Jack I

heard it all in the

news only a few
soldiers survived!"
Cried Tia's Mother.
And after that they
all went home
together.

The End.

Printed in Great Britain
by Amazon

19658875R00078